Mrs Pepperpot
AND THE Treasure

MRS PEPPERPOT AND THE TREASURE
A RED FOX BOOK 978 1 782 95576 4

First published in Great Britain by Hutchinson,
an imprint of Random House Children's Publishers UK
A Random House Group Company

Hutchinson edition published 1960
This Red Fox edition published 2013

1 3 5 7 9 10 8 6 4 2

Red Fox Books are published by Random House Children's Publishers UK,
61–63 Uxbridge Road, London W5 5SA

www.**randomhousechildrens**.co.uk
www.**randomhouse**.co.uk

Addresses for companies within The Random House Group Limited can be found at:
www.randomhouse.co.uk/offices.htm

THE RANDOM HOUSE GROUP Limited Reg. No. 954009

A CIP catalogue record for this book is available from the British Library.

Printed in China

Mrs Pepperpot
AND THE Treasure

ALF PRØYSEN ❖ **HILDA OFFEN**

RED FOX

It was a fine sunny day in January, and Mrs Pepperpot was peeling potatoes at the kitchen sink.

"Miaow!" said the cat.

"Miaow, yourself!" answered Mrs Pepperpot.

"Miaow!" said the cat again.

Mrs Pepperpot wiped her hands and knelt down beside the cat. "There's something you want to tell me, isn't there, Puss? It's too bad I can only understand you when I've shrunk to the size of a pepperpot." She stroked the cat, but Puss didn't purr, she just went on looking at her.

"Well, I can't spend all day being sorry for you, my girl," said Mrs Pepperpot, going back to the potatoes in the sink. When they were ready she put them on the stove to cook.

Puss was at the door now. "Miaow!" she said, scratching at it.

"You want to get out, do you?" said Mrs Pepperpot, and opened the door.

And just at that moment she shrank to her pepperpot size!

"About time too!" said the cat. "Now let's not waste any more time. Jump on my back and hold on tight!"

Puss bounded off with Mrs Pepperpot clinging on for all she was worth. "The first danger is just round the corner," Puss said. "So sit tight and don't say a word!"

All Mrs Pepperpot could see was a single birch tree with a couple of magpies on it. The birds seemed as big as eagles to her now and the tree was like a mountain.

"There's the cat! There's the cat!" the magpies screamed.

"Let's nip her tail! Let's pull her whiskers!" And they swooped down, skimming so close over Mrs Pepperpot's head she was nearly blown away. But Puss took no notice at all; she just kept on down the hill, and the magpies soon tired of the game.

"That's that!" said the cat. "Now we must watch out for snowballs. We have to cross the boys' playground, so if any of them aim at you, duck behind my ears and hang on!"

Mrs Pepperpot looked at the boys; she knew them all – she had often given them sweets and biscuits. *They* can't be dangerous, she said to herself.

But then she heard one of them say, "Here comes that stupid cat. Let's see who can hit it first! Come on, boys!" And they all started throwing snowballs as hard as they could.

Puss ran on till they reached a wire fence with a hole just big enough to wriggle through.

"So far, so good," she said, "but now comes the worst bit, because this is dog land, and we don't want to get caught."

Mrs Pepperpot knew the neighbour's dog quite well. She had fed him bones and scraps and he was always very friendly. We'll be all right here, she thought.

But she was wrong. Without any warning, that dog came
chasing after them in great leaps and bounds! Mrs Pepperpot
shook like a jelly when she saw his wide-open jaws all red,
with sharp, white teeth glistening in a terrifying way.

She flattened herself on the cat's back and clung on
for dear life, for Puss shot like a flash across the yard
and straight into the neighbour's barn.

"Phew!" said the cat. "That was a narrow escape! Thanks very much for coming all this way with me."

"That's all right," said Mrs Pepperpot, "but why are we here?"

"It's a surprise," said Puss. "All we have to do now is find the hidden treasure, but that means crawling through the hay. So hang on!"

And off they went again, slowly this time, for it was hard going through the prickly stalks. They seemed as big as beanpoles to Mrs Pepperpot.

The dust was terrible; it was in her eyes, her mouth, her hair, down her neck – everywhere!

"Can you see anything?" asked the cat.

"Nothing at all," said Mrs Pepperpot, for by now her eyes were completely bunged up with hayseed and dust.

"Try blinking," said the cat, "for this is where my hidden treasure is."

So Mrs Pepperpot blinked and blinked again, until she could open her eyes properly.

When she did, she was astonished; all round her shone the most wonderful jewels! Diamonds, sapphires, emeralds – they glittered in every hue!

"There you are! Didn't I tell you I had hidden treasure for you?" said the cat, but she didn't give Mrs Pepperpot time to have a closer look. "We'll have to hurry back now or your potatoes will be spoiled."

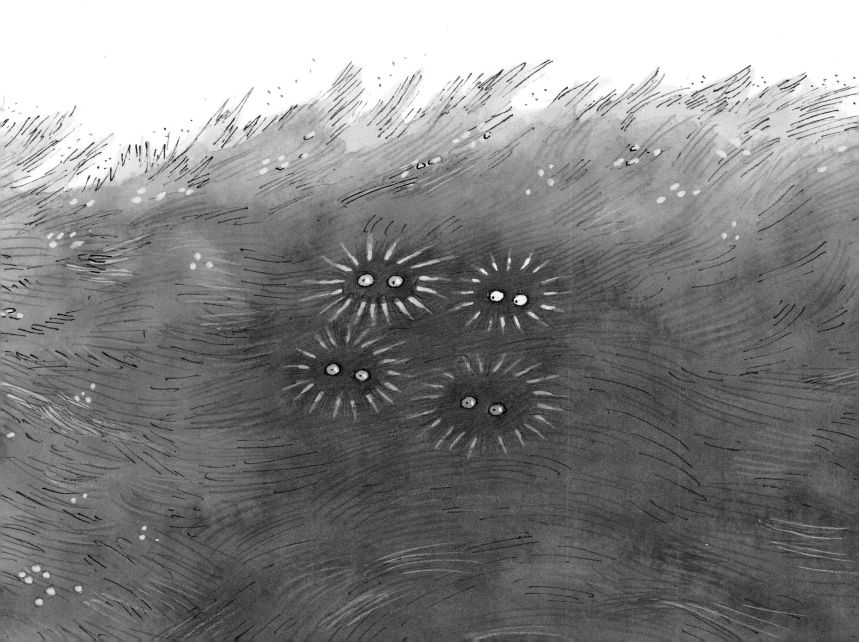

So they crawled back through the hay and, just as they came out into the daylight, Mrs Pepperpot grew to her ordinary size. She picked the cat up in her arms and walked across the yard.

The dog was there, but what a different dog! He nuzzled Mrs Pepperpot's skirt and wagged his tail in the friendliest way.

Through the gate they came to where the boys were playing. Each one of them nodded to her politely and said, "Good morning."

Then they went on up the hill, and there were the magpies in the birch tree. But not a sound came from them.

When they got to the house Mrs Pepperpot put the cat down and hurried indoors to rescue her potatoes. Then she went back down the hill, through the gate to her neighbour's yard and into the barn. She climbed over the hay till she found the spot where the hidden treasure lay.

And what d'you think it was?

Four coal-black kittens with
beautiful shining eyes!

MORE MRS PEPPERPOT BOOKS
FOR YOU TO ENJOY!

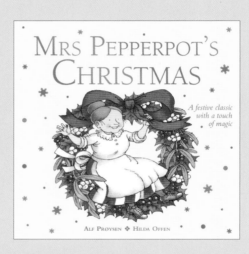

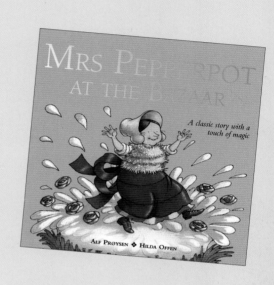

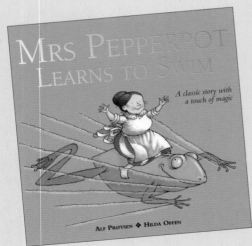

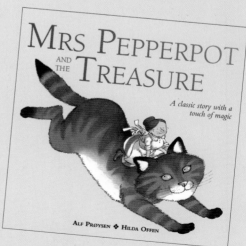